To: Ruth

♡

Angela Dusenberry

UNDERCOVER ANGELS:

Kayla's Big Move

Angela Dusenberry

Ano Klesis Publishing

www.anoklesispublishing.com

_____

Ano Klesis Publishing
www.anoklesispublishing.com

Dusenberry, Angela.
Undercover Angels: Kayla's Big Move
ISBN# 978-0-9788564-0-3

Angela Dusenberry can be contacted at
www.angeladusenberry.com.

The following trademarks were used without
permission, and UNDERCOVER ANGELS
in no way intends to portray any affiliation
with these companies: Toyota, Arbonne,
Subway, Maurices, The Spaghetti Factory,
and Safeway.

Centerville, OR is a fictional town.

Printed in the United States of America

In loving memory of Jessica Courson, who taught me what it means to love God with all of my heart.

_____

Table of Contents

Chapter 1

Fairview Academy, Here I Come!

"Are you sure I should wear the pink tank top, Mom?" Kayla asked, as Kim walked past her bedroom door.

Mom popped her head into Kayla's large room with a bay window and eyed her daughter. "I think you look fine, Hon; you had better hurry, though, it's almost time to leave." With that, she turned and walked down the stairs.

"Fine isn't good enough for my first day at a new school." Kayla frowned as she gazed into her full-length mirror. She decided against her pink tank top and threw it on the bed with the small pile accumulating there. Her purple duvet cover was almost covered with clothes that had been deemed "fine." She poured over her closet once more, and then finally decided to wear her knee length, blue corduroy skirt with her white tank top and white sandals. She added the silver heart shaped locket necklace her father had given her. A tear trickled down her cheek as she opened the locket and looked at the picture inside. The memories came unbidden…as they often did.

She remembered the day it was taken. It was April eighth, and they were at Disneyland. Dad had taken her there for her eleventh Birthday, and the two of them had their picture taken together in one of the little picture booths.

"Smile, Angel," he had said just before the flash. He had called her Angel ever since the first grade when she had come home from school crying because the other kids had made fun of her freckles. Dad said her freckles were angel kisses, and that she should always be thankful for them.

In the picture, they were both smiling, and it was evident that Kayla got her bright blue eyes from him…she missed him so much.

"I wish you could see me today, Daddy," she whispered into the mirror, "my first day of seventh grade." Somehow, she knew he was watching her from heaven. At least that is what Mom had said after the funeral. Even so, Kayla's heart hurt whenever she thought of him…especially in moments like this when she was about to experience something new. It didn't matter that almost a year had passed since her father had bravely stopped a school shooting…and in the process, lost his life. She had lost the best father a girl could have.

Kayla turned and started to clean up the pile of clothes on the bed as she thought about the past year. Mom had tried to be brave at first, but after the tragedy, she seemed more paranoid than normal. When Nana called and told them that Gramps had passed away, Kayla felt once again the turmoil and agony only those who have experienced such a loss can understand. During Gramps' funeral Mom and Nana had talked in hushed tones, and before Kayla had time to really think about what was happening, Mom announced that she would be moving Kayla and her seven-year-old brother, Cole, to Centerville, Oregon, where they would live near Nana. Even so, Mom could not fool her…she knew the real reason was that her mother was afraid. She had grown up in Centerville, and thought it was a safer place than Riverside, California. Now Kayla would have to brave a new school. She was more than a little worried about the transition.

Kayla pushed her thoughts aside, checked the silver clock in her room, and then rushed down the stairs to grab some breakfast. When she turned the corner into the kitchen, she saw Cole already gobbling down his cereal like a bear trying to get fattened up for winter. Her mother stood in their kitchen pouring her own bowl.

"Oh, honey, I hope you didn't want Fruit Loops, because I just poured the last bowl," she said with a sheepish grin on her face. She was dressed in a black skirt suit. Her brown hair was curled and piled high on her head in an elegant up-do.

"No, that's OK, Mom. I think I will just make a smoothie today. I don't want anything heavy. My stomach is kind of in knots already." Kayla got out the blender and set it on the blue, marble counter.

Mom moved over and put her arm around Kayla, "It's all going to be fine," she said as she brushed Kayla's sun highlighted brown hair out of her face and handed her the milk. Mom had a way of reading Kayla's thoughts...it was almost like their hearts had beat as one since losing her dad.

"I just hope that I fit in here. I mean, I am not used to private school. What if everyone is snobby?" Kayla said as she grabbed the bag of strawberries out of the freezer, and the rice protein from the cupboard, and then watched as they swirled together in the blender with the milk.

"I'm sure you will fit in fine," Mom said, taking a seat at the counter near Kayla. "It's not like it's a military school. It's just your basic private school where paddling is considered an acceptable form of discipline."

"What?" Kayla asked, shocked.

Mom laughed, "I'm just joking. Lighten up." Then, her voice took on a serious tone and she got that far away look in her eye. "You know, I feel better about you and Cole being in private school with all of the problems public schools are having. I couldn't bear to lose any more of my family in a shooting." Mom looked down quickly, but not before Kayla had seen the way her eyes were threatening tears.

"Mom, I miss him so much," Kayla said as tears formed in her own eyes. She heard a slight sob escape her mother as she grabbed some tissue and gave her mom a hug. Would there ever be an end to the emotional roller coaster she was on? She was so thankful that she had her mother and Cole, and now Nana.

Cole was still at the pine dining room table eating his breakfast. Kayla looked over at him and wondered how he felt about everything. At first, when their Dad had died, Kayla and Cole had bonded when they used to sit up late sharing memories together, but he seemed a lot quieter since the move. Kayla made a mental note to spend some time hanging out with him soon.

"It looks like we're both going to have to go redo our make-up now," Mom said as she took Kayla's hand and led her back up the stairs.

Kayla just loved her mom. Kim was so strong, but she also had a special sparkle even in the midst of a terrible storm. She was able to take a cloudy morning and pour sunshine into Kayla's world, which is exactly what she managed to do today. Kayla watched as her mom touched up her own make-up and then helped Kayla touch up hers; well, it was more like putting on a little more lip gloss and some blush. Since Kayla was starting seventh grade, Mom had decided to let her wear a little bit of make-up. She could wear everything except mascara, as long as she didn't end up looking like a clown. Mom was an Arbonne consultant in addition to her new job as a real estate agent, so Kayla always loved it when her mom would give her a makeover. When she was done, they both admired themselves in her mom's big closet mirror.

"If anyone doesn't like you, they're crazy!" Mom said, with a smile. It felt so good to Kayla to see the sparkle return to her mother's eyes.

Kayla went back down stairs, grabbed her smoothie, and then the three of them hustled into their blue Toyota Corolla. As her mother drove like a mad women to get them to school on time, Kayla thought about Centerville.

It was so different from her Southern California home. Kayla loved to sun bathe on the beaches that were only an hour away, or surf with her friends. Now all she had were mountains and fog…well, actually, she thought that was how Oregon would be, but so far, it had been sunny and warm. Nana said there was a lot to be enjoyed about having four distinct seasons. During the summer, her mother had even taken her and Cole to the lake a couple of times to picnic, and they did have an indoor water park. The one thing that Kayla loved the most about this new place was all of the trees. There were so many trees, even in the city. She looked out the window at the speck of blue sky peeking through the clouds and decided that even though she wasn't sure she would like Oregon, she was willing to give it a try.

Just then, her mother pulled into the school parking lot and Kayla felt the knots in her stomach return. Mom dropped her off at the front entrance of Fairview Academy. She grabbed her backpack, hopped out of the car, and threw a wave over her shoulder at Mom and Cole. As she walked through the double doors in front of her new school, she heard the bell ring.

"Oh no, I'm late already," she whispered to herself as she tried to find her first class. The school building was a lot smaller than she was used to, but it was really nice. There wasn't any graffiti on the walls, and the tan carpet looked brand new. There were still a lot of people in the halls, so Kayla figured the bell she heard was probably just a warning.

There it was, Room 202. She carefully opened the door and took a seat near the middle of the small classroom. The room was decorated with large poster size pictures of exotic places. There was a picture of a lush garden near where Kayla sat. It had a white gazebo in the center with children playing nearby in the daisies.

"You're in my seat," a brown haired boy with braces said as he pointed to Kayla. She was startled by his rudeness, and suddenly felt the urge to cry, but she quickly regained her composure.

"Oh, I'm sorry." She grabbed her backpack and found another desk in the back, near a picture of a waterfall with cascading ferns surrounding it.

"I think you're in my seat," a girl said tapping Kayla on the shoulder.

Kayla turned around and saw a red haired girl with dark green eyes. She had a warm smile and her tone was not rude at all. Kayla grabbed her backpack and stood up again, only this time she noticed that a small group of students had gathered around something on the wall. She walked over to where they stood, and that's when she realized that there was a seating chart! "Good grief," she mumbled under her breath, feeling embarrassed by her ignorance, and hoping that no one was watching her. Dad would have never gotten himself into a situation like this, she thought, he would have scoped everything out first.

It turned out that her seat was just one behind the red haired girl. She took it just as the second bell rang.

"Good morning everyone, I am Mrs. Crenshaw." Kayla looked up to see a teacher with dark brown eyes and a genuine smile. She was writing her name on the chalkboard with big swirly letters. She doesn't look like the paddling type, Kayla thought, remembering her mom's teasing.

"The first thing that we are going to do today is to choose locker partners. You may choose someone on your own, or I will assign someone to you."

A moment of panic seized Kayla. Frantically, she scanned the room for a familiar face, but she knew that no one would choose her for a locker partner. What if I get stuck with some geek? She thought, picturing herself sharing a locker with some guy who had B.O. At her old school, she had tons of friends. Suddenly she felt all alone.

"Do you want to be my locker partner?" the voice of the red haired girl in front of her broke into her nightmare.

Kayla let out a sigh. Apparently she had been holding her breath. "Thanks, I don't know anyone yet, and I was worried I would get stuck with the luck of the draw."

The red haired girl laughed, and it was like the joy of a summer day to Kayla. "My name is Sara, and although I can't guarantee to keep the locker perfectly clean, I do have a great locker mirror!"

"Great, I'm sure I'll use it all the time," Kayla said just as the teacher told them to get their stuff and follow her to their lockers.

Sara seemed really nice. Kayla got to know a little more about her while they were setting up their locker. Sara was twelve years old, a pastor's daughter, and her curly red hair was natural. Kayla confessed to Sara that at first she hadn't realized there was a seating chart, and that she thought private school people were just rude. Both girls laughed over her misunderstanding.

"No," Sara said, "people in private school are not all snobby. I think probably anywhere you go, there will be people who are rude, but I have known most of the people here forever, and most of them are nice."

Kayla couldn't help noticing the sad look in Sara's eyes as she said, "most." Kayla wondered if there was anyone in particular who was rude, but she didn't ask, because before she had the chance, Sara was flooded with other students who all seemed excited to talk to her. Kayla was pushed to the back of the circle, where she stood quietly until the bell rang.

Chapter 2
Lunchroom Friends

The next class Kayla had was gym, and luckily they didn't have to dress down. Kayla hated the uniform they had issued her when she walked in. It had a purple stripe down the leg of the shorts, and the shirt had this ugly bulldog on the front.

Kayla looked up when the gym teacher started calling out names to divide the class into squads.

"Kayla Anderson, right here." Kayla hustled to take a seat where the gym teacher had pointed, and on her way she noticed a guy that looked like he just stepped out of California with his brown hair with bleached blond streaks, blue eyes, and tan skin. Unfortunately, he didn't get called to be in her squad. She watched him walk to the other end of the gym and take a seat on the floor behind the other people already lined up there. He reminded her of the guys she used to surf with back home. She overheard someone call him Tyler. Maybe things in Oregon wouldn't be so bad after all, she thought, picturing him sitting with her at lunch, walking her to class, maybe holding her hand. She got the shivers just thinking about it.

Kayla looked around at the people in her squad. She didn't really recognize anyone. Suddenly they started cheering as the teacher called out, "Hailey Sanders." Kayla noticed how trendy Hailey was dressed as she walked confidently towards their little group, seemingly untouched by their cheers. With her fish net tights, and her western rhinestone belt, she almost looked like she was straight out of New York. But here she was, in Centerville, Oregon where people seemed to dress more conservatively than in the big cities. Her hair was short and blond with a butterfly barrette on the left side. She smiled at Kayla as she took a seat in their row on the gym floor.

Kayla tried to focus on the teacher's explanation of their upcoming activities, but Hailey kept giggling and talking to a guy behind them, and Kayla subconsciously thought maybe they were talking about her.

When the bell rang, she quickly got up and started across the shiny gym floor. As she walked, she caught a glimpse of the surfer guy. He was laughing and talking with some other guys. Kayla didn't notice the coat rack on the wall until it was too late. She ran right into the coats! Quickly she tried to pick up the ones she'd knocked to the floor before anyone noticed, but it was too late. The group of guys Tyler was with were laughing and pointing at her. She turned away from them and walked with such speed that she could have won the annual mall walk-race Nana had told her about.

As she was on her way to lunch, she stopped by her locker to see if Sara was there. Sure enough, she was just checking her hair in their locker mirror.

"Hey, mind if I sit with you at lunch?" Kayla asked, trying to catch her breath from her embarrassment.

"Sure," Sara replied with her warm smile. "What happened to you? Your face is as red as a beet."

"Oh, I just totally embarrassed myself after gym class."

"What happened?" Sara asked as they entered the lunchroom together. Kayla quickly relayed the story.

"Tyler is a cool guy," Sara said. "I've known him forever. He goes to my church, plus we've gone to school since like kindergarten. Maybe I could introduce you to him."

"No, thanks," Kayla said. "I don't think I ever want to meet him now after what just happened." She quickly changed the subject. "We had better find a seat." She pointed to the small lunchroom, which was filling up quickly.

"Oh, I usually sit outside when it is warm," Sara said. So, they both went through the cafeteria line and then Kayla followed Sara out into the courtyard. It was a grassy area in between several buildings. There were picnic tables surrounding the lawn on the concrete, but most of them were already   full.

"What is this stuff?" Kayla asked as they chose a spot near the edge of the concrete in the sunshine.

"It's called spaghetti-pizza," Sara said with a giggle. "It is one of the chef's favorites. We had it all of the time last year. She just mashes down the spaghetti and uses it for the pizza crust. We usually have it the day after we have spaghetti."

"That is so gross."

"I always say that the food here is like God, the same yesterday, today, and forever." With that, both girls burst out laughing.

"Well, I think I am going to make a mental note to pack my lunches from now on," Kayla said.

"Oh, look," Sara pointed to a tall gangly boy walking into the courtyard by himself. "He was at youth group last week. I think he's new in town. Do you mind if I invite him to sit with us?"

"Of course not," Kayla said, excited to meet more people.

"Josh, over here," Sara called, waving her hands in the air. Slowly, Josh made his way over to them. His eyes were all squinty from the glare of the sun. "Hi, this is my friend, Kayla," Sara said introducing the two of them.

"Nice to meet you," he said, "and you're Sara, right?"

"Yeah, I'm impressed you remembered."

"So," Kayla broke into the conversation, "you're new in town too? Where are you from?"

"Oh, my family moved here from Colorado. We just opened a new hamburger place called Main Street Grill." Josh took a seat on the other side of Sara. "You'll have to check it out. We have local bands play on Friday and Saturday nights."

"That sounds like fun," Sara said, "You should have our youth pastor, Jimmy, play. His band is really cool."

"I'll talk to my dad about it," Josh said just before he took a bite of his huge sandwich.

"So, you both go to the same church?" Kayla asked. "I think we are going to start going to church with my grandma soon. We have just been too busy unpacking to go, and my mom works late at the office a lot." Somehow, Kayla felt like she was making excuses, even though no one said anything.

"What does your dad do?" Sara asked.

Kayla looked down at the grass. "He used to be a policeman," she said slowly, "but he passed away last March."

Sara's face turned ashen, and Josh just stared at her with his mouth gaping open. (Luckily, he had swallowed the bite in his mouth).

"Oh, my…" Sara said, "I'm so sorry."

"It's OK," Kayla said, trying to lighten the mood. This was one of the hardest parts about losing a parent…knowing how to deal with people's reactions to the news. "He was a hero. He got shot during a school shooting. He jumped the guy with the gun, and got shot in the process."

"You don't have to talk about it, if you don't want to," Sara said, "I can't imagine losing one of my parents. It must be so hard."

"It's alright. I'm doing much better now than when it first happened."

"Is your mom doing OK?" Josh asked, "I mean it has to be really hard for her to suddenly be a single mom, with all of the bills and everything."

"Oh, she's doing great," Kayla suddenly felt a burst of pride for Mom. "After Dad died, she took classes to be a real estate agent, and she's sold make-up through Arbonne for as long as I can remember."

"Arbonne, what kind of make-up line is that?" Sara asked as she tried to bat away a honey bee.

"It's pretty cool, and it's all botanically based," Kayla said with a smile, glad the conversation was shifting to a more comfortable topic.

"Alright, alright," Josh said, "I'm not going to sit with you guys anymore if you start talking about girly stuff." Sara and Kayla both laughed.

"Does that mean that you are planning on sitting with us tomorrow?" Sara asked.

Josh's face turned red, as he answered, "Only if you don't talk about girly stuff."

Just then, several more people joined them, three more girls, and two boys. Kayla once again felt left out. They had obviously known each other for years. Kayla found herself feeling angry at Sara. She glanced over at Josh. He was just eating his sandwich with a content look on his face. Kayla tried to involve herself in her own lunch, but something about spaghetti-pizza just wasn't inspiring.

Sara seemed so nice, but then she would almost ignore Kayla when her other friends came around. Kayla checked her thoughts. So far, Sara was the only one who had befriended her, and she should be thankful.

When lunch was over, they all went to their lockers. Kayla walked with Sara to history class, hoping she could sit next to her, but there another seating chart. She was stuck in the very front of the class, and Sara was way in the back.

She would have asked to switch seats, but Mr. Bradford looked like he belonged in the military, with his strong set jaw and bald head. Maybe her mom was telling the truth about this private school actually paddling kids. Kayla wouldn't put it past this teacher. She decided that she would just sit up front for the time being.

Just before the second bell rang, Hailey, the girl from Kayla's squad in gym class, and a bunch of other kids came running into the room. One of the guys almost knocked over the globe near the door. Mr. Bradford looked up from his desk and simply said, "Hailey, take your seat up front, and I expect you to walk." When Hailey and her friends were seated, he told everyone to take out their books and then they all took turns reading aloud.

At the end of class, he divided the students into groups to work on the questions at the end of the section they had just read. Hailey was in Kayla's group. Kayla took a piece of paper out of her notebook, but Hailey waved it away. "We don't study unless we have to," she said. "I'd rather talk. So, where are you from?"

Kayla slowly put away her piece of paper, "Riverside, California," she said.

"That is so cool that you are from Southern California. I love California. My dad lives there."

"Yeah, I miss the beach already." Kayla said, suddenly feeling a little homesick, and missing not only the beach, but all of her friends as well.

"It must be hard moving to a new town," Hailey said. "Hey, would you like to sit with me tomorrow at lunch? I'll introduce you to my group."

"Sure," Kayla said just before the bell rang. She liked the idea of actually getting introduced to a group, instead of just being overlooked.

As she left the classroom, she stopped to talk to Sara.

"Did you finish the questions?" Sara asked.

"No, we just talked the whole time."

"Man, that's a bummer, now you have homework. Well, I guess if I was new, I would probably rather get to know people and just do the assignment later too."

Just then, Hailey walked by.

"Bye Hailey," Kayla said. "See you tomorrow."

"Bye," Hailey said, but her voice sounded strained, and she gave Kayla a quizzical look as she passed by.

That was strange, Kayla thought, as she walked with Sara to their locker. She carefully loaded her blue backpack with her history book and her binder, and then she realized something. She had made it through her first day at Fairview Academy. So far, so good, she thought.

Chapter 3
Nana's Flower Shop

After school, Kayla couldn't wait to get over to help Nana out at her florist shop on Main Street. Kayla waited in front of her school for Mom to pick her up for what seemed like forever. The sun was shining, and the air smelled fresh from the pine trees near where she stood. Almost all of the other students were gone before Kayla finally spotted their blue Toyota Corolla pull into the school parking lot. Mom drove to the back of the school to pick up Cole first, and then she pulled up to where Kayla waited. Kayla hopped in.

"How was school?" Mom asked as she accelerated to the edge of the parking lot, and then pulled out into traffic. Kayla told her about how she met Sara and Josh, and how she embarrassed herself in gym class. Cole was kind of quiet. He didn't mention making any new friends.

They drove past a local park, and Kayla noticed a huge skateboarding area out her window.

"Mom, could we stop here and skate!" Cole said, changing instantly from his quiet mood into the enthusiastic little brother Kayla had always adored.

"Not today," Mom said, as they were waiting the second time for the same light. "I only have twenty minutes to get Kayla over to help Nana, you to daycare, and back to the office to finish up." Cole looked crushed, and Mom looked frazzled. Maybe she wasn't holding up as well as Kayla had thought.

"I could take him tomorrow after school," Kayla offered.

"I don't know," Mom said with hesitancy in her voice. "It is dangerous for the two of you to be out alone."

Kayla didn't mention the fact that they used to always be allowed to go to the park alone before Dad had passed away. Mom was just being paranoid now. "I am twelve years old," Kayla said instead. "That's legal babysitting age. Just think of how much stress it would take off of you if you let us walk home from school by ourselves, and I could watch Cole until you got off of work. It would be perfect."

"I'll think about it," Mom said, which basically meant "no" coming from her. Kayla sighed, and then it was quiet the rest of the way to Nana's.

Mom pulled up to the curb in front of Main Street Flowers, and Kayla carefully climbed out. She walked to the glass door and gently pushed it open. The bells hanging from the door jingled, and Kayla took in a deep breath as the smell of fresh roses and carnations drifted to her.

"Oh, hi dear," Nana said as she put down the flower arrangement she was working on and came over to give Kayla a hug. Kayla noticed that Nana was wearing her floral print flood pants. She just loved how Nana always seemed so young. Her hair was blond with only a little gray, and her skin was a beautiful tan from all of her gardening.

"How was school?" she asked with that caring smile of hers.

"Well, I made a couple of friends," Kayla informed her. "One of them is a pastor's daughter." Kayla knew that would impress Nana. She always seemed to care about where people stood with God.

"That's great, hon. I'm glad that you are choosing friends so wisely," Nana said, trying to stuff a stray daisy into the arrangement she was working on. "A lot of times," Nana went on, "we don't realize how much our friends affect us, especially when we are in school. I have been praying that you and your brother would make just the right friends when you moved here. It must be hard starting all over. I'm so proud of you."

"You know something else you could pray for, Nana," Kayla said carefully, feeling like Nana had some kind of special standing with God, "that Mom would stop being so overprotective. She won't even let me and Cole walk home from school by ourselves, and I know that shuttling us around so much is stressing her out."

"Oh, Kayla, I would be glad to pray for that. And don't you worry, dear. Your mom will come around, you'll see."

As they were finishing up the daisy bouquet, the shop got kind of busy. A young man came in to buy a dozen roses for his fiancé. He was tall, and had dark skin and dark eyes. Kayla tried to picture what his fiancé might look like. An elderly lady stopped by to pick up her order for her husband's funeral. There were three huge floral arrangements, and the sight of them made Kayla remember all too well the funerals she had recently been to.

"Nana," Kayla said after she had helped the elderly lady out to her car, "do you still miss Grandpa every day?"

Nana's expression turned somber. "Yes, I guess you could say that. We were together for thirty eight years, and you know as the Bible says, 'the two become one.' It is a strange mystery, but I felt like half of me was missing when Samuel passed away."

Kayla couldn't help thinking Nana sounded a little lonely. She might have lost her dad, but

Nana had lost her whole family. Kayla suddenly felt glad they had moved to Oregon. Nana needed family.

"I love you Nana," Kayla said and gave Nana an impulsive hug.

"Oh, Kayla, I love you too," Nana said, turning from the flower arrangement she was working on and focusing all of her attention on Kayla. "One thing I have learned from losing your Grandpa is that you have to be thankful for the people you have in your life, and never take anyone for granted. God has blessed me with so many wonderful people, like you and Cole, and your Mom, and all of the ladies from church."

Just then, another customer walked in. It was a tall brown haired lady and a little girl. Kayla helped fill up five birthday balloons.

"We've got to hurry and get to the Grill," the lady said to her daughter, "Dad and Josh are waiting there for us."

The Grill! Kayla had forgotten all about the grill on Main Street that Josh had told her about. This must be his mom and sister.

As soon as they left, Kayla peeked outside and watched where they went. The Grill was just up the block and across the street.

"Have you been to that new grill yet?" Kayla asked Nana.

"Not yet," Nana said. "What have you heard about it?"

"A guy I met from school told me all about it." Kayla went on, "His parents own it, and he said they have local bands play there on Friday and Saturday nights. Maybe we could all go this weekend."

"That's a great idea, Kayla. I'll call your mom soon and arrange everything."

Kayla's time with Nana always seemed to go by so quickly. Before she knew it, five o' clock had come and it was time for them to close up shop. Nana drove her home and dropped her off at their white two-story house. Even though her house was average size, it seemed so big in comparison to the trailer Nana lived in all alone.

When Kayla walked in, she could hear the shower running upstairs. Mom liked to take hot showers when she was stressed out. The kitchen still had their dirty dishes from breakfast. Kayla ran up to her room, dropped off her backpack, and then popped her head into Cole's room. He was building a fort out of blocks.

"Hey, little bro, you want to help me surprise Mom and make dinner?"

When he saw Kayla he smiled. "You'll show me what to do?" he asked, always weary of the kitchen.

"Sure, we'll make something simple like spaghetti."

They both raced into the kitchen, and by the time they heard Mom's footsteps on the wooden stairs, dinner was on the stove and the dishes were all done.

A look of relief flooded Mom's face as she rounded the corner and came into the kitchen.

"I set the table, and buttered the bread, and washed the vegetables for the salad, and helped to dry the dishes," Cole said excitedly.

"Thank you both so much," Mom said as they all sat down at the table. She said grace, and then they enjoyed their spaghetti.

"This is how spaghetti should be," Kayla said. "I like spaghetti, and I like pizza, but I don't think the combo works too well." She went on to explain how their cafeteria cooks were a little too creative for her taste. Mom laughed and said she would add sandwich stuff to her grocery list.

Chapter 4

Poisoned

"I thought pre-algebra would be hard, but not this hard," Kayla said to Sara just before they got to their locker at lunchtime on Wednesday. "Thirty problems for homework on the first day of class—I worked for the last half hour and only got seven done. I thought block scheduling was supposed to give you more time in class to finish your work."

"Welcome to private school," Sara said as she dug for her sack lunch.

"Hey, Kayla," Hailey called out to her as she approached the two of them. "Are you still planning on sitting with me?"

"Yeah sure," Kayla said. "Save us a seat."

"Oh," Hailey glanced deliberately in Sara's direction. "I think there is only room for you."

Kayla stared at Hailey dumbfounded, but Sara spoke up before she had a chance to object.

"That's OK," Sara said, with complete calmness in her voice. "I'm at a really good part in my book, and I think I'll just find a nice spot in the sun and see how it ends." With that, she flashed both of them her big smile, and then turned and walked away.

Hailey linked arms with Kayla as though they had been friends for years, and led her to a table near the middle of the cafeteria. Kayla recognized a couple of the faces as Hailey introduced her to the group. There was Kyle, a guy with wavy black hair and glasses she recognized from her pre-algebra class. He looked kind of like the musician type. There was also a guy named Zack she recognized as the guy Hailey had been talking to from their gym squad. He fit the part of a jock so well; Kayla had almost laughed the first time she saw him. The two other girls Hailey introduced her to she hadn't seen yet.

Come to find out they were eighth graders: Janea and Trish. Janea had long blond hair and light blue eyes. She wore a red shirt with a trendy denim skirt. Trish had short brown hair. Kayla noticed she was wearing a lot of rings and bracelets. She liked the silver charm bracelet on her left hand.

As Kayla sat back and ate her lunch, she started to feel less homesick. She was so easily accepted into this group. She wondered to herself why she had ever worried about making friends.

She looked out the window to see where Sara was, expecting to see her reading her book, but instead she saw her eating lunch surrounded by guys! Well, at least two guys, but the thing that intrigued Kayla was that Tyler was one of them. Of course Josh was the other. Sara threw her head back and laughed at something Tyler was saying. What were they talking about? Kayla wondered.

"Aren't you locker partners with that Sara girl?" Trish said breaking into Kayla's thoughts and making her feel like it was a crime to be Sara's locker partner.

"She is for now," Hailey answered for her, "but next year she can be my locker partner. She hasn't heard the lowdown on Sara yet."

"What are you talking about?" Kayla asked innocently.

"About how her father is actually a murderer," Trish said. The way she narrowed her eyes into little slivers that looked like almonds made Kayla shiver.

"Yeah," Hailey joined in, "well, at least he tried to murder someone. Have you met Justin yet?"

"Who's Justin?" Kayla asked.

"He's Sara's older brother," Hailey said. "He's the one Pastor Ryan tried to kill!" Hailey's voice took on a hushed tone. "It was seven years ago. Pastor Ryan poisoned him because he didn't want him to take over his church someday. But, it didn't work out that way because the ambulance came and the paramedics saved his life." Hailey crossed her arms for added emphasis, "Sara claims he had an allergic reaction to a bee sting, but I saw him. His face was all swollen. I've been stung by bees plenty of times, but nothing like that ever happens." Hailey finished her story with deep authority in her voice.

"That's a stupid story," Kyle said while he ate his roast beef sandwich. "You know you just made that up."

"No she didn't," Janea defended, "It's the truth."

"Yeah, you are just defending Sara," Hailey said with a disgusted look, "because you used to have a crush on her in fourth grade."

Zack just seemed to ignore the whole thing. With his head down, he just kept eating his chips. Crunch, crunch, crunch Kayla's head started to pound with every bite he took.

Kayla had to do something fast. She quickly searched her lunch for a topic idea. "I sure miss our California fruit," she said as she pulled out her apple.

At first everyone just stared at her goofy smile, and then Hailey spoke up, "Yeah, everything about California is better than this place."

"What about their silly fruit inspection booths?" Kyle said. "There's nothing more annoying than having a bag full of fresh cherries and having to give them away."

"Yeah," Janea said, and have you ever noticed they never ask for the same thing? I think they just ask you for whatever they happen to be hungry for."

"One time," Trish said, "we were going on a family vacation to the coast, and of course, to get to the closest beach you have to go down into California and then back up into Oregon again. Well, we had all of these apples, and luckily we remembered before we got to the border. Dad made us eat all of those apples, and do you know what happened when we got to the boarder? The guy asked if we had any plants or animals! Here Dad was all ready to hand him our apple cores, and he asks for plants or animals." She shook her head for emphasis, and her short hair flipped back and forth with the movement. "What would they do to you if you did have your dog with you? Put him in some sort of anti-Oregon decontamination dip?" With that, everyone laughed.

"Speaking of food, have you guys been to that new Grill yet?" Zack asked, "I hear they have some killer food.

"Does Sara's dad run it?" Hailey asked, and everyone burst out laughing again.

After lunch, Kayla still had a slight headache, and her stomach was in knots again. She didn't like what Hailey had said about Sara. Surely it wasn't true, but then again, she didn't know Sara all that well. As she walked to Spanish class, she pondered Hailey's words and tried to dismiss them as gossip. To her relief, neither Hailey nor Sara was in her class. She noticed with a little smile that Tyler, the cute guy from her gym class, sat behind her and there wasn't even a seating chart. She decided Spanish was going to be one of her favorite classes.

Chapter 5
Shopping Adventures

After school on Friday, Mom picked up Kayla, and to her surprise, announced they were going to go on a shopping spree. First they dropped Cole off at Nana's, and then headed to Centerville Mall.

The mall was a little bit smaller than the one she was used to in Riverside, but it did have a lot of cool stores. They found a parking spot near the main entrance, and then made their way into the mall.

As they walked past one of the make-up booths, in the first department store, Mom said, "Oh that reminds me, I need to start scheduling some more make-up parties soon. A woman's work is never done!"

"Mom," Kayla said with a slight roll of her eyes. "We're supposed to be having a fun shopping day. You can't think about work right now."

"I know, I know. I'm sorry."

"Look Mom, they have khaki trench coats!" Kayla said as she searched for a size small, and then slipped it on over her clothes.

"It fits nice," Mom said eyeing her.

"I'm glad most of the school year is during the winter," Kayla said as she walked over to the mirror on the wall. "I don't think I could stand the no shorts dress code if school was in the summer like back home." She did a few turns to admire the jacket.

"You would get used to it," Mom said. "Private school is not the only place you will have to deal with a dress code. Most offices have dress codes. As a matter of fact, almost any job you get will have some sort of dress code."

"I guess you're right."

"At least they don't make you wear a uniform."

"Thank goodness," Kayla said.

"Hey, what do you think about this top?" Mom said, holding up a shirt that looked like it was directly out of the army, but the camouflage was blue.

"I don't think it is quite my style," Kayla said, trying not to hurt Mom's feelings. They looked around a little longer, and then got the trench coat for Kayla and some black pants for Mom.

Next they went to a couple of Mom's favorite stores, and then to Maurices. Kayla got a new denim skirt at Maurices. It was short and faded. She also got a sparkly white top to go with it, and a pair of brown boots just for fun.

"Let's go to the food court," Mom suggested after they purchased the boots. "I'm starving."

As they made their way to the food court, Mom asked, "Where do you want to eat?"

Without hesitating, Kayla said, "Subway!"

As they got in the Subway line, Mom pointed to the hot dog place next to them and said, "Speaking of uniforms."

Kayla turned to look. The guy at the counter was wearing a huge hot dog hat! "No kidding," Kayla said, laughing. "At least I don't have to wear something like that to school."

"Are you ready," the lady at the counter asked Mom when they got to the front of the line.

"Yes, I'll have a turkey salad," she said.

"I'll have a chicken sub on wheat," Kayla said, and then proceeded to let the lady know what veggies she wanted.

Mom paid for their food, and then they both filled up their water cups and found a seat in the crowded food court near the yogurt place. Kayla couldn't help feeling lonely even though there were people all around her. It was strange to go to the mall and not run into anyone she knew.

"Do you think you can eat some yogurt?" Mom asked when Kayla was almost finished with her sandwich.

"No, I'm stuffed," Kayla said, "plus, I want to check out the store we passed on our way here called Dianne's."

"Alright then," Mom said as Kayla helped her clear their table. "I want to go there too. I think my best friend from high school might be the owner. I haven't talked to her for years, but I heard she had her own store."

Dianne's was a medium sized store in the center of the mall. The windows were glass, and the store was brightly lit with antique lights. It kind of reminded Kayla of the Spaghetti Factory. The carpet was red, and there were several three-way mirrors scattered throughout the store.

Kayla immediately fell in love with the clothes. They were stylish, but kind of unique. She picked up a pair of blue leather pants, and a rhinestone tank top. The tank top was on clearance, but it was still thirty dollars, and the pants were over a hundred. Kayla grabbed several other items, and then headed for the dressing room while Mom looked around.

"Hi," Kayla heard a lady say to Mom. "Is there anything I can help you with?"

"Dianne?" Mom said. "So you are the owner."

"Kim? I can't believe it's you!"

Kayla stopped paying attention to their conversation and tried on the blue pants. They were a little bit too big. Suddenly, her ears perked up when she heard Dianne mention Fairview Academy.

"My daughter goes there too," Mom said. "Maybe they have met."

When Kayla came out of the dressing room, Dianne and Mom were still talking. They ware both smiling and reminiscing about their high school days.

"This is my daughter, Kayla," Mom said in a formal introduction. Kayla took a good look at Dianne. Kayla immediately noticed her "big hair." It was bleached blond and didn't have any shine to it, but it was fluffed up with what looked like a lot of backcombing and hair spray. She wore pointy heels and a tight black skirt.

"Have you met my daughter?" Dianne asked Kayla. "Her name is Hailey Sanders."

Kayla couldn't believe it. Hailey's mom and her mom were good friends! No wonder she and Hailey had hit it off right away. "Actually, I sat with her at lunch this week," Kayla replied.

"So, you're friends," Dianne said. "Well then, I guess I'll be seeing you around. Are you ready to make your purchase?"

Kayla handed her the rhinestone tank, and then found a purse and several necklaces she also wanted. She put the blue pants back while Mom paid for her little pile on the counter.

"That was so much fun," Mom said as they walked to their car. She had a far away look in her eye like she was still thinking about her high school days with Diane, and Kayla could tell she was not expecting an answer. Man, if only Sara and Hailey weren't enemies, Kayla thought. What had gone on between them anyway? There must be some way to be friends with both girls. Kayla felt like she was caught in a spider's web.

That night Kayla's best friend from California called.

"Jerusha, it's so good to hear your voice!" Kayla said. "I miss you so much." Jerusha had been Kayla's best friend since second grade. She was a gorgeous black girl with a perfect complexion and long shiny hair. Her dad worked in the police department where Kayla's dad had worked.

"I miss you too sister. This year has just been terrible so far," Jerusha said, making Kayla feel bad for deserting her just before seventh grade. "Everyone is coupled up already, and it is only the first week of school! All of our friends are still nice to me and all, but I feel like a third wheel."

"I guess I'm not the only one with problems then," Kayla said. She told Jerusha about how she had made friends with two girls who seemed to be enemies, and she didn't even know why.

"Hang in there," Jerusha said, "I'm sure things will get better."

"You too," Kayla said as she got a call on the other line. "Hello, oh, hi Nana, I've got Jerusha on the other line, but we were just about to get off, hold on." Kayla said good-bye to Jerusha, and then gave Mom the phone. Kayla worked on her homework for a while, and pretty soon, Mom popped her head into her room and announced they were all going to go to Main Street Grill on Saturday night.

All right! Kayla thought. She went to her closet to pick out an outfit to wear.

Chapter 6

Main Street Grill

When Kayla heard the doorbell ring, she raced down the stairs to greet Nana. She had decided to wear her favorite jeans and a screen tee that said, "Surf's up." She wore a brown belt, her brown boots from Maurices, and a baseball cap.

"You look adorable," Nana said after she came in. "Where are your Mom and Cole?"

"Oh, Mom's almost ready, and Cole is…" before Kayla could finish her sentence, Cole came bounding down the stairs and threw both arms around Nana.

Kayla wondered if maybe she had just been imagining that Cole had changed. He seemed like lately he was more himself. Mom followed a couple of minutes later, and then they all made their way to the car.

They could hear the music from Main Street Grill all of the way down the street where they found a parking spot almost a block away. Kayla was so excited. She wondered if she would see anyone that she recognized from school.

A man who looked like he was in his thirties opened the door for them. He gave Mom a big smile, and it made Kayla feel strange. People didn't smile at Mom like that when Dad was with them. For the first time, Kayla thought about the possibility of Mom getting remarried. She didn't like the idea, not one bit.

As they walked through the glass double doors, Kayla looked around. The Grill was decorated Hawaiian style with palm trees, and surfboards. Tahitian dance music was playing over the sound system. A young waitress asked them how many were in their party, and then seated them in a booth near the back. There was a stage in the front of the room, and it looked like they were just getting set up for the concert.

"Would you like anything to drink?" their waitress asked. Kayla looked up, and quickly recognized the woman as Josh's mom.

"Just water for now," Mom said as Josh's mom passed out their menus.

"Aren't you the people from the flower shop?" she asked them.

"Yes," Nana said, "I own Main Street Flowers, and this is my granddaughter, Kayla. She helps me there sometimes."

"Well, I'm Rachel Coffman," Josh's mom said, and then Mom introduced herself and Cole before Mrs. Coffman left to give them a few minutes to look over the menu.

"I'm going to have a cheese burger with fries and a root beer," Nana said when she came back to take their order.

Kayla ordered a veggie burger, French fries, and a Diet Coke. Cole and Mom both got hamburgers and milk shakes.

The band started up while they were waiting for their food. Kayla was surprised to see Kyle, the guy from Hailey's group with black wavy hair and glasses, playing base guitar. The band was actually pretty good. Kayla scanned the crowd for Hailey, and sure enough, she was sitting at a table up front, by the stage.

After their food came, Kayla asked if she could go and join Hailey's table.

"Sure," Mom said. "I'm glad you're fitting in so well here already."

Hailey was sitting with Janea and Trisha. They were laughing and joking about something when Kayla walked up.

"Hey, take a seat," Hailey said as she motioned to the seat next to her. Her shoulder length, blond hair was crimped and pinned up on both sides with rhinestone barrettes. She looked like a model straight out of her mom's store. "Isn't Kyle's band cool?"

"Yeah," Kayla said, "I didn't realize he was in a band." The music was not quite Kayla's style. They had kind of a punk/rock sound. She couldn't understand the words they were singing very well, but they were obviously talented musicians.

"I like your shirt," Janea said to Kayla. "I love screen tees." Janea was wearing pinstriped flood pants with a hot pink sweater-tank top. Trisha was wearing black and silver as usual, but her hair was a slight shade of purple now. She must have dyed it since school on Friday.

Before long, Zack joined their table, and when Kyle's band took a break, he joined them as well. They all complimented Kyle on his music, and then laughed and talked together until he had to start playing again. Kayla caught Hailey staring at him while he walked back up to the stage. I wonder if Hailey has a crush on him, Kayla thought. He did look pretty cute up on stage with his wavy black hair and mysterious eyes.

The rest of the night Hailey entertained their little group with her boisterous personality. Kayla hadn't laughed so much in a long time. It was fun to feel like she belonged. She was almost sad when Mom came to tell her it was time to go home.

"Bye guys," Kayla said as she turned to leave. "See ya."

"See ya," they all echoed back.

The rest of the weekend was pretty uneventful. They didn't go to church because they still had some unpacking to do, but Mom promised Nana they would try to go to church on Wednesday night.

Monday at school, Kayla followed Sara out into the courtyard for lunch. She saw Hailey and her crowd at their usual table, but they didn't seem to notice her. Just as they got situated on the grass, a familiar voice made Kayla look up.

"I see you decided to grace us with your presence today," Tyler said as Josh sat down next to Sara.

"Well, I uh," Kayla stammered, not quite remembering what the question was. The only thing she could think of was...I'm going to meet Tyler. Secretly, he was the reason she had chosen to sit with Sara instead of Hailey. Finally her brain kicked in, and she answered him. "What are you talking about?"

"Well, I thought maybe you were too good for us," he said. "You know, hanging with Hailey and all."

"Oh Ty, give it a rest," Sara said. "She doesn't have any reason not to like Hailey, and we certainly aren't going to give her one." With that, Tyler sat down next to Kayla and began looking through her lunch.

"What are you doing?" she asked, shocked.

"Oh, I'm just checking to see if you have anything good."

"Get out of here," Kayla said with mock anger as she gave his hand a little slap.

"I'm Tyler by the way," he said, holding out the hand Kayla hadn't slapped. "I think I am the one you were staring at when you just about took out the coat wall." He raised his eyebrows as he spoke while a mischievous smile crept across his tan face.

Kayla could feel her face turn red. She playfully slapped his other hand away, refusing to shake it. "I'm Kayla, I'm new, so be nice to me," she said.

Tyler laughed, and finally he took the focus of the conversation off of her. "Wasn't church good on Sunday?" asked Josh and Sara.

"Yeah, Pastor Ryan really hit home that point about God's love for us," Josh said.

"I think he has been thinking a lot about love lately since it was my Mom's and his seventeenth anniversary last week," Sara said.

Kayla felt left out. Here they all went to the same church, and they sounded like they actually enjoyed it. Kayla couldn't figure out why. She and Jerusha used to go to church together back in Riverside, but they would have never talked about the sermon during lunch at school. Church was just something you did. It wasn't fun. You just sat there while the pastor yelled about how wrong sin was.

The bell rang, breaking into Kayla's thoughts. They all gathered up their things, and then headed for their lockers.

"See you later," Tyler said to the two girls as he followed Josh down the hall.

"Would you like to come over for dinner Thursday night?" Sara asked while Kayla got out her Spanish books.

"Sure, that sounds like fun," Kayla answered.

"I'll have to check with my parents first, but I'm pretty sure it will be fine."

"Let me know," Kayla said as she turned to leave. "I have an orthodontist appointment tomorrow," Sara called after her, but I'll let you know for sure during history."

Chapter 7

Safeway

To Kayla's surprise, Tuesday afternoon Mr. Bradford announced that they were going to play a game.

"I thought because all of you have been working so hard we could take this whole period to play history trivia," he said. "The two students with the highest scores will be let out of class ten minutes early."

The whole class let out a cheer. Kayla loved games and she had a good memory, so it came as no surprise to her when she got almost every question right. As a matter of fact, she was winning! Actually, Hailey was coming in first, but Kayla noticed her book just "happened" to be open on the floor. She rolled her eyes when she saw it.

"Well, It's time for our two top scorers to get out of class," Mr. Bradford announced at ten till three. "See you guys on Thursday."

Everyone clapped as Hailey and Kayla both gathered up their books and headed for the door.

"My parents said dinner is fine," Sara whispered to Kayla as they passed her seat.

"What was she talking about?" Hailey asked Kayla with a quizzical look, as they walked to their lockers.

"Oh, she invited me over to dinner this Thursday," Kayla said, not sure she wanted to hear Hailey's reaction.

"You can't go over there!" Hailey exclaimed. "Pastor Ryan will probably try to poison you."

"Hailey, that's ridiculous," Kayla said.

"Fine, get poisoned, but don't say I didn't warn you," Hailey said. Then she jumped to another subject, catching Kayla off guard. "Hey, do you want to walk to Safeway with me to get a soda? I don't have to be to volleyball practice until three-thirty."

Kayla checked her watch to make sure she still had enough time before Mom came to pick her up. It was eight minutes till three, and her mom was usually at least ten minutes late. "Sure," she said.

The parking lot was quiet when they walked through it. Kayla was used to it being noisy, with parents either picking up or dropping off their kids. It seemed kind of eerie with the parking lot so empty.

It was still warm outside, but there was a slight chill in the air. Kayla wished she had brought her sweater.

She glanced over at Hailey, and she realized this was the first time they had been alone together. She wondered if Hailey would be a little bit deeper one on one.

"Justin, Sara's brother called me the other night," Hailey said. Kayla thought maybe she was actually about to share some deep secret, but then she went on. "He is a total dork. He has chubby cheeks. I gave him the total brush off, I mean like, one word answers to everything he said. It was so funny because he was way nervous. I don't think I'll have to worry about him calling me again." Hailey's short hair flipped in the breeze as she spoke animatedly, using hand gestures to demonstrate her point.

Kayla thought carefully about what to say, "You know, you may regret being rude to him someday."

"What ever for," Hailey said flippantly, "like I said, he is a dork."

"What if he suddenly gets really cute," Kayla said, and having fun with her "what if," she went on. "He might end up being the captain of the football team, or something. What if you change your mind and decide you totally like this Justin guy, but it's too late, and he never forgives you for how you treated him. It could happed you know."

"Whatever." Hailey reached in her red purse, "You want some gum?" she asked.

"Sure."

"So, do you like anyone?" Hailey asked.

Kayla thought of Tyler. "I think I kind of have a crush on Tyler," she said, feeling her cheeks blush.

"Tyler Newton?" Hailey said with obvious disgust. "He is a nerd. I have known him since kindergarten, and he has always been this chunky kid. Come to think of it, he doesn't seem chunky this year," Hailey said as she appeared to be contemplating Tyler's current appearance. "But he is still a nerd," she finished just as they walked into Safeway. Kayla let the subject drop just as Hailey's jaw did the same.

"Oh my gosh," she said as she grabbed Kayla's arm and pulled her behind aisle three. "There's Pastor Ryan."

Both girls crouched down and pretended to look at something on the bottom shelf.

"I was wondering...poison...in stock?" they couldn't make out every word he asked the clerk, but it didn't look too good.

"Yes, it's on aisle seven." She answered him.

"Hailey gave Kayla a knowing look. They stayed where they were while Pastor Ryan went to aisle seven, brought his purchase to the counter, and then left the store.

"Did you see him?" Hailey asked. "See, I told you he is planning to poison you! I wouldn't go over to his house for dinner for a million bucks."

As Kayla followed Hailey to the self-serve soda fountain, she started to have second thoughts about dinner at the Smith's house.

Hailey purchased her soda, and the girls quickly walked back to the school.

Kayla didn't have very much time to think about dinner at Sara's. When they turned the corner into the school parking lot, there was their familiar Toyota Corolla with Cole in the back seat and Mom in the front seat with a frown on her face.

Chapter 8
Heart to Heart

Kayla carefully opened the front passenger door and climbed in next to Mom. Mom just stared at her, waiting for an explanation. Kayla tried to divert her attention by quickly changing the subject and speaking at a rapid pace. "I just saw Pastor Ryan buying poison at the store. Hailey says he is a murderer, and I can't go over to their house for dinner on Thursday. I just can't."

"Whoa," Mom said holding up both hands and giving Kayla one of her just a minute looks. "What were you doing at the store? Don't tell me you walked there by yourself. Do you know how dangerous that is?"

"Mom, I went with Hailey. We got out of class early because we won the history jeopardy game."

Mom had finally started driving. She was taking a right out of the driveway as she said, "I don't like you running all over town with God knows who."

"Hailey is Dianne's daughter," Kayla said, trying everything she could to get out from under Mom's paranoid lecture. "You used to let us go places by ourselves all of the time. Kayla turned and looked directly at Mom. It was not customary in her family to disagree with a parent, but Kayla decided to brave the worst and speak what was on her mind. "Mom, you can't keep me in a bullet proof box for the rest of my life." She paused and let out a big sigh. The sound of the engine suddenly seemed loud in comparison to the silence of that moment. Kayla pressed on, "Dad always said you have to live life, and not always be worried something bad will happen. Remember the story he told us about the father who wanted to protect his children from flying rocks while he mowed the lawn? He put his kids in the shop, but one got hit by a flying rock that went right through a crack in the wall and he had to go to the hospital anyway." Kayla waited for the lecture she knew she deserved for talking so disrespectfully, but Mom did not let out a sound. Instead, Kayla saw a tiny tear trickle down her cheek. No one spoke for the rest of the ride home. Kayla felt awful. Even Cole just stared out the window.

As soon as they got home, Mom went straight to her bedroom without a word. Cole went upstairs too, and Kayla was left standing in the living room by herself. "Now how am I going to get out of going to Sara's house for dinner?" she asked herself. As she voiced the thought, she remembered eating lunch with Sara and how nice Sara had been. Surely her dad couldn't be a murderer, but then, she had seen him buying poison. What other reason would he be buying poison? Kayla sure couldn't think of any.

After about half an hour, Kayla knocked lightly on Mom's door, and then walked in. Mom was sitting on her bed with the family Bible open. Tears stained her cheeks, and she still hadn't changed out of her work clothes.

She patted a spot on the bed next to her, and Kayla took a seat.

"Mom, I'm sorry about what I said earlier," Kayla began. "I was just so upset about seeing Pastor Ryan … please don't make me go over there for dinner, please." Kayla had both of her hands intertwined as she proceeded to beg.

Mom let out a faint laugh. Kayla stared at her trying to figure out what was funny.

"Kayla, I can't believe you just gave me a lecture about not being paranoid, and now you actually believe Pastor Ryan is a murderer!" Mom shook her head but then her eyes turned serious. She gently stroked Kayla's hair. "When your father died, I was so upset. I kept thinking about all of the things I should have done differently. I should have made him get a different job. I should have insisted we move to a safer community. I should have made him wear a bullet proof vest." She let out a little laugh. "But you know the truth is, being a police officer is what John wanted to be, and I know for a fact he would have willingly given his life to stop that school shooting."

Now Kayla started to tear up. It was so hard losing Dad.

"Today you have helped me to realize I can't keep you and Cole locked up all of your lives. You are right, you are old enough to walk to the store in broad daylight, and I certainly don't want you to start being paranoid too. Pastor Ryan, a murderer, good grief." Mom handed Kayla some Kleenex. "And another thing, I think I am going to make more of an effort to get this family to church!"

Wow, that came out of nowhere, Kayla thought. "Does this mean I have to go over to Sara's for dinner?"

Mom grabbed a pillow and whacked Kayla over the head with it, "yes!"

Kayla grabbed a pillow and tried to get in a few blows. Before she knew it, they were both laughing, and their hair had enough static electricity to light up Las Vegas.

Right before Kayla left Mom's room, Mom caught her by the arm and said, "And you had better not ever talk back to me like you did in the car again."

"You've got it," Kayla said as she smiled.

Kayla spent the rest of the night doing homework and trying not to think about dinner at Sara's.

The next day at school, she tried to avoid both Sara and Hailey. It was hard since she had so many classes with both of them. In Pre-Algebra, she noticed Sara's brother, the guy Hailey had been rude to on the phone. Kayla couldn't understand why Hailey would be so rude to him. He seemed nice enough. He was even kind of cute, plus he was an eighth grader. Sara was lucky to have an older brother like him.

Kayla's thoughts turned back to Hailey. She was an adventure waiting to happen, which made her fun to hang out with, but Kayla just couldn't figure out her actions sometimes. Maybe being an only child had something to do with it.

The rest of the day seemed to fly by. Before Kayla knew it, school was out, and she was up in her room getting ready for church. It was the first time they were able to go with Nana. Things had been so busy since the move they hadn't had time for church, but things were different now. Mom had decided to make it a priority.

Kayla pulled on her pink skirt with little white daises, and her white sparkle top. She stared in her closet for a while before deciding to wear her straw wedge sandals, and her hoop earrings. With one last glance in her mirror, she was ready. She grabbed her white purse, and ran downstairs to get something to eat before it was time to leave.

They picked up Nana on the way, and Kayla almost swallowed her gum when she heard Nana say the pastor's name was Ryan Smith. They were going to Sara's church! How could Mom take them there? Kayla was certain she wouldn't be able to concentrate on his sermon. She would be picturing him trying to poison people.

"I'm sure you two will love your youth groups," Nana said, breaking into Kayla's thoughts.

So, she wouldn't have to listen to Pastor Ryan's sermon after all. Kayla let her shoulders relax a little bit, but before she knew it, she was being hustled into the church building.

They dropped Cole off first at his class, and Kayla couldn't help noticing the sad look on his face. Her thoughts didn't dwell on him for long though. Before she knew it, she was in the youth room.

Kayla stared at the room in amazement. There was a mural that started on one wall and continued all around the room. By the door where she walked in there was a snowboarder, and then the snow turned into the ocean. The whole right side of the room looked like the beach scene she was used to, complete with surfers. She quickly scanned the room to see if Sara was there. Sure enough, she was standing near the surfing corner of the room talking to a bunch of girls. Kayla was trying to decide what to do when a familiar voice caught her attention.

"Hi Kayla," Tyler said. "So I guess your grandma goes to Centerville Christian Fellowship."

"Yeah," she said just as another familiar face joined them. "I didn't know you went here," Josh said.

"Neither did I until tonight," Kayla said with a shy grin. Before the conversation continued any further, a young man with wavy brown hair and sideburns called for everyone's attention.

"He's the youth pastor, Jimmy," Tyler whispered into her ear as they all took a seat on the floor. Kayla was surprised when Jimmy started playing the guitar and everyone started singing. There was so much enthusiasm in this group. People were closing their eyes and lifting their hands. The songs had an upbeat sound to them. They were not at all like the hymns she was used to singing; although, a lot of the words were the same.

After worship she was really surprised when Jimmy said they were continuing through the book of James. He told everyone to open their Bibles to chapter two. It seemed like everyone had his or her own Bible. Kayla wished she had brought her student Bible, but it was still tucked away in a box somewhere. She decided she would make sure she unpacked the rest of her room soon so she could find it. Also, she had never had a teacher teach through a whole book of the Bible before. She was used to topical teachings that were found here and there. She sat up straight to listen, almost forgetting about Tyler, Josh, and Sara.

Jimmy started reading, "My brothers, as believers in our glorious Lord Jesus Christ, don't show favoritism." The chapter went on to talk about how Christians should treat people equally, whether they were rich or poor. Kayla was fascinated at how Jimmy made the Bible seem so interesting. When he got to verse fourteen, "What good is it, my brothers, if a man claims to have faith but has no deeds?" Kayla settled in for a lecture on how Christians should do good deeds, but she was surprised by what Jimmy actually said.

"Good deeds are not something that can be mustered up," he said. "Nor are they something that can earn forgiveness. Good deeds are evidence of true faith." Kayla was a little bit flustered. She always thought her good deeds kind of outweighed the bad things she did.

When Jimmy got to verse nineteen, Kayla was horrified. "You believe that there is one God. Good! Even the demons believe that—and shudder." Suddenly Kayla felt like she was in some kind of horror film. *Maybe there is more to being a Christian than just believing in God's existence,* she thought, stunned.

Jimmy went on, "Being a Christian is having the kind of belief that is proven through actions. If you knew there was a bomb in your house, ready to go off at any minute, you would leave the building immediately. If you told me you believed there was a bomb in your house, about to go off, but you just sat on your couch watching

T.V., I would have to question whether or not you really believed there was a bomb.   In the same way, if you really believe God loves you and died on the cross to pay the price for your sins; you will make Him your Lord and do what He says."

When the service got out, Kayla's head was spinning.   What could it all mean?   She numbly said goodbye to Tyler and Josh and then headed to the car.

As they rode home, Nana asked them all what they thought.

Mom answered her first, "Well, I was a little surprised at first because it was not exactly what I was expecting, but I really enjoyed it.   It was especially nice to see so many young people."

Kayla looked over at Cole as he answered. "My youth group was cool.   We got to play a bunch of games, and my teacher was nice.   She gave me a snickers bar because I could recite the memory verse."   Kayla noticed his dimple as he smiled.   She was glad to see her little brother happy again.

Mom cleared her throat and began to speak again, "The teaching was about not being afraid, and trusting in God."   She glanced at Kayla in the rearview mirror.   "I know I told you yesterday that I have been paranoid lately, but now I think it is time for me to do more than just admit it isn't good to be afraid.   She took a deep breath, and Kayla could see her chest rise and fall slowly from the front seat before she spoke again.   "I think it is time

I gave the two of you more freedom. If you want to start walking home from school with Cole, you can, and you can take him to the skate park tomorrow if you still want to. After all, you are twelve, and that is legally old enough to baby sit."

Cole let out a scream of excitement, and Kayla was so excited that Mom was finally giving her more freedom, she almost forgot about youth group and Jimmy's troubling teaching.

Chapter 9
Cheated

Thursday morning at school, Kayla felt distracted. Her mind kept wondering, and during P.E. she kept missing the goal in their soccer game.

Hailey had detention during lunch, so Kayla sat with Sara.

"I'm sorry I didn't get to say 'hi' at church last night," Sara said as she dug into her sack lunch and pulled out her strawberry yogurt. "Amber was having a crisis at public school, and she needed me to be there for her." Kayla figured Amber must be one of the girls Sara was talking to while she was admiring the mural on the wall.

"That's OK." Kayla said. "I had to leave right after church anyway."

"So, what did you think of youth group?" Sara asked.

"Well," Kayla said, choosing her words carefully. "I thought Jimmy was cool."

"Oh yeah, totally," Sara answered with her usual enthusiasm as she pulled out her spoon and started to open her yogurt. "Is your family going to start going to CCF? Or were you just church shopping last night?"

"I think we are going to start going there. My grandma has been going there for years." Kayla tried to hide her fears and confusion about going to Sara's church as she spoke.

"Cool," Sara said. "Jimmy is the best youth pastor ever. He is always planning fun trips. I think he is planning a snowboarding trip to Mt. Ashland as soon as it opens. Do you snow board?"

"I have been once or twice at Big Bear," Kayla said, glad the conversation was going in a lighthearted direction. "Surfing was way more my thing, because it is kind of a year round sport in Southern Cal."

Before Kayla knew it, the bell rang, and she was off to history class, glad the school day was almost over. She took her spot next to Hailey, and after the second bell rang, Mr. Bradford handed out a pop quiz. Kayla joined in as there was a collective groan, and then she got out her pen and began to answer the questions. Her mind started to wander. She thought about how exciting it was to get her freedom back, but then her mind drifted to the teaching at youth group. What was it Jimmy had said? Something about good works not outweighing the bad. That part about even the demons believing in God made her feel insecure. She wasn't sure who she was anymore. If doing good deeds didn't really matter, then why should she try so hard to be a good kid? Just then she heard a quiet, "pssst." She turned to her right and saw Hailey mouth, "I need to see your answers. Move your arm." Kayla hesitated, and then she casually moved her arm and turned her paper so Hailey could see it. What could it hurt? She reasoned.

Just as she was finishing up her quiz, she saw Mr. Bradford's looming presence right in front of her. She looked up at him as he slipped her paper off of her desk then took Hailey's as well.

"I'll need to see you two ladies after class," He said before he went back to his desk.

After class, Kayla stood in front of his desk with her head down and Hailey at her side.

"Cheating will not be tolerated at Fairview Academy," He said with such sternness in his voice it made Kayla shudder.

"You will both receive an 'F' on this quiz and detention tomorrow at lunch. And..." he looked directly at Kayla. She tried to look him in the eye, but was unable to. "Kayla, your new seat will be in the back of the class next to Sara Smith."

As they walked from the room, Kayla felt terrible. She had always been a "good" kid. She had never been in trouble with a teacher before.

As soon as they turned the corner and were out of Mr. Bradford's hearing, Hailey began fuming. "I can't believe the nerve of him," she said with clenched fists. "I'll think of some way we can get him back."

Kayla thought it was strange for Hailey to be mad at Mr. Bradford. Hailey was the one who cheated. Kayla was a little upset at her for getting them both into trouble. She turned from Hailey, quickly put her books in her locker, and headed for her bike. She wasn't about to let Hailey, Mr. Bradford, or Jimmy's teaching ruin her day. She was going to take Cole to the skate park, all by herself.

"Hey, Cole," Kayla said when she saw him waiting for her by her bike. "Are you ready to check out the skate park?"

"Yeah," he answered, but he didn't seem as excited as Kayla had thought he would be.

"Race you there!" Kayla said, trying to cheer him up as she mounted her bike and started heading out of the school parking lot. He hopped on his skateboard and took off after her.

When they reached the park, Cole got right to work practicing his stunts. Kayla found a spot in the shade to watch. She sat down and leaned her back against a big oak tree. As she reached into her backpack to get out her apple, she thought about what a beautiful day it was to come to the skate park. The sun was shining, and there was a slight breeze. She started to think about her new school and her new friends. She felt a pain of guilt as she thought about letting Hailey cheat off of her. Life seemed so confusing since Dad had passed away. He was her rock, the one who kept everything stable for her. Now, she was living in a new place, with new people, but no father.

Just as she was deep in thought, she heard a voice above her.

"Hey, what are you doing here?" Tyler asked as he stood in front of her with his hands in the pockets of his khaki pants.

"I'm here with my little brother, Cole. He's right there practicing his jumps," she said as she pointed in Cole's direction. A slight shiver went through her body at seeing him so suddenly.

"No way. He is good for his age! I didn't know he was your brother. I have been watching him. He could use a few pointers, but he's got the basic stuff down really well."

"Yeah," Kayla replied, feeling more at ease. She suddenly swelled with pride in her little brother. "He used to be even better. My dad taught him a lot…before he passed away." She wasn't sure why she was telling him about Dad. Maybe it was just that she had so much on her mind, or that she didn't have anyone else to talk to. Well, she was close to Mom, and Nana, but sometimes it was just nice to talk to someone her own age. "Cole didn't skate at all for a long time after it happened," she continued. "He just started skating again before the move. I'm glad he wanted to come today. He's been so quiet lately. I think he is having a hard time making new friends."

"I'm so sorry to hear that," he said with genuine compassion as he ran his fingers through his bleached blond hair. "It must be really hard for you too."

There was a moment of silence. Kayla heard the leaves of the tree above her swaying in the wind, and then he spoke again. "I know what I can do to help. I have a little brother about the same age as yours, and he loves to skate too. I'll run home and get him." With that, he waved over his shoulder and was off. Kayla could hardly believe how nice he was to her. He was by far the cutest boy she had seen at school, and here he was doing personal favors for her.

Before long, he was back with his little brother, Shane. Kayla watched from the shade of the Oak tree as Tyler began to engage the two younger boys in what looked like a mini skate lesson. Before long, all three of them were laughing.

When it was time to go, Kayla walked over to where the boys were skating. Cole flashed her one of his huge smiles. It was the kind she had almost forgotten, it had been so long.

"Just a few more minutes," he said in a pleading voice.

"O.K.," Kayla answered, "but we've got to get going soon. I'm going over to Sara's house for dinner tonight."

Tyler overheard her and said, "Tell Sara 'hi' for me."

"Sure," Kayla said, almost feeling jealous. "Thanks for helping Cole. It means a lot to me."

"Anytime," Tyler said with a smile that made Kayla blush.

"Well, we've got to go," Kayla said as Cole came over to them. "See you later."

"Bye Tyler, bye Shane," Cole said as they turned to leave. Kayla rode her bike home with a smile on her face. Somehow, she didn't feel so bad about the history test anymore. You never know what a day will bring, she thought.

Chapter 10

Adventures in Babysitting

Kayla put her key in the lock and gently pushed open their front door. The house seemed strangely quiet inside without Mom.

"When will Mom be home?" Cole asked, and Kayla could tell from the frown on his face that he felt the same emptiness she did.

"In a couple of hours," Kayla answered him. "Why don't we do our homework until she gets here?"

"I need help with mine today," he said.

Kayla wasn't sure what she should do. She was supposed to go to Sara's for dinner, so she needed to work on her own homework now.

"Can't Mom help you later, after dinner?"

"No," Cole said as they both made their way upstairs. "She said I needed to get it done before she gets off work." He screwed up his face into a frown before adding, "We have to go to the grocery store tonight."

"Oh," Kayla said. Suddenly this whole babysitting thing didn't seem so glamorous anymore. She had been hoping to get her homework done quickly, and then download some new music to her iPod. Now she would have to rush just to get her homework done.

She went to her room to put away her backpack before settling down in a beanbag chair in Cole's room. She glanced at the walls in his room, and was once again thankful he ended up with the blue room and not her. There were still a few boxes of toys yet to be unpacked, but Cole had done a pretty good job of decorating his room, considering it had blue walls. Mom said she would get him a wallpaper boarder with soccer balls on it when she had time, which, lately, seemed like never. Cole had put up two posters of skaters, and she noticed he had already set up the train set Dad had gotten him last Christmas.

"So, what do you need help with?" Kayla asked him after he had gotten situated at his desk.

"Math," he said wrinkling up his nose.

"Let's get started then," Kayla said, just as the phone rang. She ran to Mom's room to answer it. "Hello," she said and then heard Jerusha's familiar voice on the other end of the line. "Hey sis," Jerusha said, "What are you up to?"

"Oh, I wish I had time to talk, but I have to help Cole with his homework." Kayla felt annoyed again. She would have loved a chat with Jerusha.

"I'm sorry; I'll call you back later then."

"Thanks," Kayla said, glad to know her friend wouldn't have any hard feelings.

She went back to Cole's room bringing the cordless phone with her this time in case there were any more calls. She helped Cole for the next twenty minutes or so trying not to think about what she would rather be doing. Luckily she was a good student and a patient teacher, but when Cole announced he needed a bathroom break, Kayla was in no hurry to make him stay and finish his assignment. "O.K." she told him as he scurried from the room.

She was trying to figure out how she would explain borrowing in subtraction when the phone rang again. This time it was Nana.

"I was just wondering how you were doing," Nana said, but she sounded kind of lonely to Kayla.

"We're doing fine, what are you up to today?"

"Oh, nothing really. I'm just at home." Kayla thought of the retirement mobile home park Nana lived in. It was always so quiet. "I decided to go home early from the shop today. Carol wants more hours, so I think I will start taking the afternoons off."

Just then, Kayla heard a loud scream. Nana must have heard it too, because Kayla heard her ask, "What's wrong," as she quickly ran to the bathroom. Cole was sprawled on the floor and blood was running down his cheek. Kayla felt queasy when she saw the big gash on his forehead.

"Oh my gosh! Cole, what happened?" She said trying to calm him, but feeling panic rise in her chest. That's when she noticed the toilet had overflowed and there was water everywhere.

"I slipped... and hit my head... on this," Cole said in between sobs as he pointed to the bathroom cabinet.

"Kayla, Kayla," she heard a faint voice call her name. She relaxed a little when she remembered Nana was still on the phone.

"Nana, Cole slipped in the bathroom, and it looks like he needs stitches," she cried into the phone.

"I'll be right there," Nana said and then Kayla heard the dial tone.

Cole's clothes were all wet. Kayla tried to help him up, but soon realized she needed to put something on his wound or he would get blood everywhere. She grabbed the first aid kit out of the bathroom cupboard and gave him a thick piece of gauze.

Her head was spinning. What should I do next? She thought.

"Am I going to be O.K.?" Cole asked barely above a whisper.

Kayla tried to regain her composure for his sake. "You're going to be just fine. First we need to get you to your room so we can get you some dry pants, and then we need to get downstairs to meet Nana."

Ten minutes later, Nana knocked on the door and then rushed Cole off to the hospital. Kayla went back upstairs to clean up the bathroom. Some afternoon, she thought with the mop and mop bucket in tow. It was the grossest job sopping up murky toilet water. By the time she was finished and had changed her own clothes, she was exhausted. She didn't know how many more afternoons like this she could handle.

She was just finishing up her homework when she heard Mom come home. She quickly relayed the gruesome afternoon to her. Mom's face went pale when Kayla told her Cole was at the hospital with Nana.

"Why didn't you call me?"

Kayla wasn't even sure of that herself. Why hadn't she called Mom? "I um, I guess I didn't want to disturb you at work," she said.

"Kayla, I'm your mom. You should have called me!"

Just then, Nana pulled up. Mom and Kayla both rushed outside to see Cole. He had a big smile on his face and a lollipop in his hand.

"I got five stitches. Does that mean I get out of going to the grocery store?"

Everyone laughed, as they all went back into the house.

"Aren't you supposed to go to Sara's house for dinner tonight?" Mom asked when everything had settled down.

"Oh, I almost forgot! Is it still O.K. if I go?" Kayla wasn't sure if Mom still wanted to give her freedom after what happened, and she wasn't even sure if she wanted to go.

Mom only hesitated for a second before answering, "Of course."

Kayla felt kind of bad not telling Mom about cheating in history, but she quickly brushed aside the thought. Now wasn't a good time after all. Mom was already dealing with a lot. She didn't need to add any extra worries; at least that's what Kayla told herself, as she got ready to go to Sara's.

Chapter 11
Diner at Sara's

By the time Kayla hopped on her red mountain bike and headed for Sara's house, she was feeling a lot better. She was so glad Cole was all right, but she was a little frustrated with the whole afternoon. She didn't know if she could stand another day like this, but she didn't want things to go back to the way they were either. Even with all of the afternoon's craziness, Mom hadn't looked as stressed as usual. Surely there was some way to save both of their sanity. There just had to be.

Kayla was so caught up in thought as she turned onto Sara's street that she almost forgot about the possibility of dinner being life threatening.

She hesitated for a moment when she got to the yellow and white house that was Sara's. It was a one-story house unlike her two-story one, but it had a cute yard complete with a birdbath. She deposited her bike in the driveway and then walked up the stone path that led to the door. After Kayla rang the doorbell, a small woman with short blond hair opened the door.

"You must be Kayla," she said, and Kayla noticed this woman had the same warm smile as Sara. "I'm Elizabeth, but everyone calls me Liz. Come on in, Sara is down the hall in her bedroom. Dinner will be ready in just a few minutes."

Kayla walked past Liz and headed toward the hall, to where she was pointing. The inside of the house was simple yet homey. She liked the brick fireplace in the corner. There was a family picture on the hearth, and Kayla noticed Pastor Ryan had fiery red hair like Sara's. Suddenly she felt a little awkward being in their home. The afternoon had been so busy she had almost forgotten about cheating on their history quiz. Now, she started to feel guilty as she made her way down the hall to Sara's room.

"Hey, how are you doing?" Sara asked as she finished putting some photo's in an album.

"Fine, is that a picture of Tyler?" Kayla asked trying not to sound too interested as she plopped down on the bed beside Sara.

"Yeah, it was on the Mexico trip this summer," Sara said casually. "We visited an orphanage down there and helped work for a week."

"Wow, that sounds like a lot of fun," Kayla said, glad Sara wasn't bringing up history class. "I lived only a couple of hours from Mexico, but I have never been. Oh, by the way, Tyler told me to tell you 'hi.'"

"When did you talk to him?"

"Oh, he was at the skate park when I took Cole there today."

"So, do you have a crush on him?" Sara asked with a big smile and a knowing look.

Kayla blushed. "No," she said. "I just, think he's nice. Well, O.K., I think he's cute too."

"He's a great guy," Sara said just as Liz popped her head in the doorway and announced dinner was ready.

Sara made her way to her seat at the dinner table. Kayla followed her and took the seat to her right. She was introduced to Pastor Ryan and Justin, Sara's older brother.

So far so good, she thought. She stared at Justin, and once again wondered why Hailey would think he was a dork. He had light blond hair, and blue eyes. They weren't as bright as Kayla's, but they were handsome.

"Oh, no, I forgot the lemonade!" Liz said as she started to get up.

Pastor Ryan quickly stood and said, "No hun, you've been working hard. I'll get it." With that, he got up from the table and made his way into the kitchen.

Kayla felt a moment of panic seize her. Pastor Ryan was alone in the kitchen with their drinks! Suddenly, Hailey's words came to her, "I'm warning you, he will poison you." She tried to push the thought from her mind. The seconds she sat at the table seemed like hours. Finally, she decided she had to do something. She had to see what Pastor Ryan was up to. She quickly got up from the table. "He will need help carrying all of those glasses," she said before anyone could object.

As she turned the corner into the kitchen, she saw him dumping some white powdery stuff into a glass of lemonade.

"What are you doing?" Kayla said in a voice that caused Pastor Ryan to spin around with a surprised look on his face. She quickly changed her tone to one of nonchalance and repeated her question. "What are you doing? Can I help?"

"I'm just about finished. I'm just adding some sugar," he said with a confused look on his face. "Did Liz send you in here to help?"

"Uh, no, I just thought you might need some help," Kayla said, knowing she wasn't telling the complete truth. She saw the sugar container Pastor Ryan placed back in the cupboard. It certainly looked like it was really sugar.

Pastor Ryan handed her several glasses, and she realized she had no choice but to follow him back into the dining room. She took her seat at the table, but she had inwardly resolved not to try the lemonade.

"Let's pray," Pastor Ryan said, and everyone bowed their heads and closed their eyes. "God, we thank You so much for all You have provided for us, and we pray that tonight You would be with those who are less fortunate than us. Thank You for Sara's new friend, Kayla. We pray You would bless her, and help her as she adjusts to a new town. In Jesus name, Amen."

When Pastor Ryan was praying, Kayla felt drawn to his voice. It had been a long time since she had heard Dad say grace, and the way Pastor Ryan talked to God seemed so simple. It was almost like God was right there with them, not some great power way out in space.

When Kayla opened her eyes, she quickly glanced around the table. Sara's family seemed so complete. She felt a slight pang of jealousy.

"So, what did you do when you got out of class early the other day?" Sara asked, after everyone had been dished up.

Kayla swallowed the bite of salad she had in her mouth and answered, "I went to Safeway with Hailey because she wanted to get a soda."

"Oh, that reminds me," Pastor Ryan said to Liz, "I got that rat poison you wanted me to pick

79

up. Our rat problem should be over before you know it."

"Ryan!" Liz exclaimed, "Rats are not a dinner topic."

Kayla didn't pay much attention to the good-natured family quarrel about what was appropriate conversation for the dinner table. She was too occupied with her own thoughts. If Pastor Ryan was buying poison to kill the rats, then he wasn't planning to kill her at all. Kayla looked at Pastor Ryan. He was laughing and she caught him give Justin a wink. Kayla couldn't help but notice the love this family obviously shared, but the best part was they were willing to share it with her. She let out a sigh as she thought about how silly she had been, and then she took a big drink of her lemonade.

Chapter 12

Nana's Home

Later, after Sara's mom gave Kayla and her bike a ride home, she went up to her room to call Jerusha back. So much had happened. She needed to talk to her closest friend.

"Hello," Jerusha said into the phone after three rings.

"Hi, it's me," Kayla said.

"Well, it's about time you called me back, girl. I have big news, I have a boyfriend."

"You do?" Kayla could feel the corners of her mouth curl up into a smile as she thought about how just last week Jerusha was outraged because everyone else was paring up. Apparently it wasn't so bad if you were the one doing the paring.

"He's so cute. He's black, but he has blue eyes."

"He sounds cute to me," Kayla said.

"So has anyone asked you out yet?"

"No, but this guy named Tyler hung out with me today when I was at the skate park with Cole."

"So, it sounds like things are looking up for you," Jerusha said.

Suddenly Kayla felt a heaviness settle over her, as she realized that things were not looking up at all. She started to tell Jerusha about church and the confusing things Jimmy had said, but somehow she couldn't bring herself to talk about it. She decided to tell her about babysitting Cole instead.

"That's crazy," Jerusha said after Kayla told her the whole Cole saga. "You've got to come up with a plan to get out of watching him every day."

"I know, but what am I going to do? Mom is stressed out trying to take care of both of us by herself."

"What about your Grandma?" Jerusha asked, "Isn't she available?"

"Not really, she owns a flower shop."

"Oh," was all Jerusha could say.

Kayla was feeling frustrated. She felt like all they were doing was pooling their ignorance and coming up with nothing.

After she said goodbye, she plopped herself onto her bed. She was already dreading tomorrow. Spending the entire seventh grade watching Cole everyday didn't seem too appealing. She pondered her options once again. What was it Nana had said today? It was something about not working in the afternoons anymore. A picture of Nana all alone in her quiet mobile home park ran through Kayla's mind, and suddenly an idea began to form. She knew what the solution was, if only Mom would go for it.

She knocked quietly on Mom's door then let herself in after she heard the familiar, "It's open."

"What's up?" Mom asked as Kayla took a seat on her bed. Mom finished combing her hair, and then took a seat beside Kayla.

"Well, I've been thinking…" Kayla began.

"Oh no," Mom teased.

"No seriously," Kayla said trying to sound as grown up as she could. "Things have been kind of crazy lately."

Mom got a frown on her face. "Are you talking about what happened today with Cole? Have you changed your mind about watching him after school?"

"No, I mean yeah, I mean, I think we need more help."

"Whoa, hold on," Mom said, "I am not about to hire some stranger to watch you guys here. The thought of that just creeps me out."

Kayla almost let out a chuckle at the look of horror on Mom's face. "That's not what I meant. I was thinking maybe Nana could move in with us. It must be so lonely for her in that trailer park all by herself."

Mom let out a sigh, "Oh, I'm glad you weren't suggesting I hire some crazy teenager, but I think Nana moving in here is almost as far fetched. She wouldn't want to have us underfoot all of the time, and besides, she has her floral shop to keep her busy."

Kayla felt all hope drain out of her. "Can't we at least ask her?" She said with her most pleading look. "She said she is going to stop working afternoons in the flower shop, and I know she needs us as much as we need her."

"Well, I have to confess I have thought about it more than once since we moved here. I just don't want her to feel like she has to."

"I know she wants to. I can tell by the look in her eye every time she drops me off here. She looks sad, like she wished she didn't have to leave."

"Oh, alright, I guess it doesn't hurt to ask." Mom held up one finger and pointed it at Kayla as she added, "But don't get your hopes up. We are not going to pressure her."

Chapter 13
Toilet Papering

During detention on Friday, Hailey passed Kayla a note that said: "I have a plan to get back at Mr. Bradford. You will need to spend the night at my house tonight. I'll explain it all then."

Kayla reluctantly asked for permission from Mom to spend the night at Hailey's house. Somehow deep in her gut she knew Hailey meant trouble, but at the same time, she felt compelled to go. Hailey also meant adventure.

Mom was overjoyed Hailey had invited Kayla over. "I think it is so cute you and Hailey are friends. I remember when Dianne and I were young. We would have so much fun together." Mom went on and on. By the time they got in the car to go to Hailey's, Kayla was practically nauseous from hearing all about the good old days.

Cole was at a friend's house, so it was just the two of them. When they pulled up in front of Hailey's house, Kayla's mouth dropped open in surprise. It was a mansion. There was a man-made waterfall near the front of the house, and the house itself must have been at least three stories tall.

Mom helped Kayla get her sleeping bag and her backpack out of the trunk, and then they headed for the front door. When Kayla rang the doorbell, a woman in a black apron dress opened the door.

"You must be Kayla," she said. "Hailey is expecting you." Kayla was a little bit surprised to find out just how wealthy Hailey was. She has a maid! She thought as they followed the tall woman through the long hallway leading into the living room. Kayla took in her surroundings while they waited for Hailey. The house was decorated Victorian style, complete with red rugs laid out on the wood floors and antique pictures on the wall. The decorations were beautiful, but the house didn't have a homey feel like Sara's did. It seemed almost eerie.

Soon, Hailey was explaining to Mom that her mother would be working late, and she was sorry she couldn't be there to meet her. As soon as Mom left, Hailey got right down to business.

"Trisha and Janea will be here any minute," Hailey excitedly told Kayla. "Trisha got her older brother, Dave, to drive us tonight, and we are going to pick up the guys on the way."

"Guys? On the way to where?" Kayla asked, not sure she really wanted to know.

"Oh, to toilet paper Mr. Bradford's house, of course. I found out where his house was yesterday when I followed him home from school. It is the perfect way to get him back for giving us detention."

Kayla didn't know what to do. She realized she didn't have much choice; she had to go along with Hailey's plan. It couldn't be that bad, could it? It might even be some fun. "Won't your mom have something to say about this?" Kayla asked innocently.

"Mom, she's never around. She went to this fashion show in Florida, and she won't be back until Monday. And Chelsea, our maid, never pays any attention to me anyway. I just told your mom she was working late, so she wouldn't worry. I mean she is working late... until Monday." Hailey laughed at her little white lie, but Kayla was starting to feel sick inside. She wasn't comfortable with people lying to Mom.

Kayla heard the doorbell ring, and before she knew it, she was watching Runaway Bride with Trisha, Janea, and Hailey. They proceeded to watch two other movies and eat a whole pizza before they pretended to go to bed at twelve o'clock.

Gathered in Hailey's room, the girls all dressed in black pants, black turtlenecks, and black boots. They tried to be patient while they waited for the clock to strike two. Kayla was catching the excitement. She had never toilet papered someone's house before. She only wished it didn't have to be a teacher, and not out of revenge. Nevertheless, at two a.m. she snuck out of the house with the other three girls to meet Dave in his green Jeep.

He drove like a crazy person, and Kayla was nervous they would get pulled over and get busted for being out after curfew. When they got to Kyle Roster's house, Dave slowed to a stop. Both Kyle and Zack were waiting for them. Kyle was dressed in camouflage pants with a black long sleeved shirt and a black bandana. Zack had on his black warm-up pants with his Blazer's sweatshirt. Both guys got in the car. It was packed with all seven of them. All four girls were in the back, and the three guys were up front.

Kayla's pulse began to race, as they got closer to Mr. Bradford's house. Dave parked across the street in a little alleyway, and Hailey and her group made their way to the front yard. Kayla could see pretty well because of the streetlights, and she hoped no one would spot them. Mr. Bradford's house looked spooky as dark shadows played across the greenish-blue siding from the tall shrubs that lined his yard. The girls began to wind the toilet paper around the trees as Hailey directed the boys to go into the backyard.

Before long, the house and the yard were covered in toilet paper. They must have used fifteen or twenty rolls. Just as Kayla thought they were about to leave, Hailey ran back to the car and brought back a carton of eggs. Kayla looked at her in horror, as she started throwing them at the house. Kyle saw her too, and he tried to stop her. "Hailey, that isn't cool," he said, grabbing her arm.

"Fine," she said as she jerked her arm free. "Wait in the jeep then."

Kayla watched from the safety of the bushes while Kyle went to the jeep. Hailey kept throwing eggs at the house one after another. Trisha and Janea joined in, and Kayla noticed Zack sneak off to the jeep. She felt a shiver shake her whole body. The night air was cold against her face. She looked up at the sky. It seemed so huge. She suddenly felt insignificant and all alone. This was certainly an adventure, but it somehow didn't seem as fun as she had hoped it would be.

Suddenly, the porch light came on, and Janea let out a high-pitched scream.

"Someone's coming," Hailey whispered. "Let's get out of here!" All of the girls started running for the car, but before anyone knew what was happening, Mr. Bradford came out of his house with a shotgun! Kayla was almost to the car when she heard Trisha scream. She looked back just in time to see her fall to the ground.

Kayla watched in horror as Mr. Bradford caught Trisha by the back of her jacket while she was trying to get up. She started kicking and squirming until Mr. Bradford's gun slipped from his hand and he had to let go of her to catch it.

"Get in the Jeep," Hailey said, freeing Kayla from her trance. Hailey pushed her into the backseat and then climbed in after her. Dave had already started the engine, and he started driving before Janea and Trisha even reached them. They kind of tumbled in on top of Hailey, and Kayla tried to help hold them in while Hailey shut the door.

Kayla's heart was beating so hard; it felt like it was shaking her whole body.

"Whew!" Dave yelled once everyone was safely in his jeep. "That was close."

"Are you O.K.?" Kayla asked Trisha, "I thought maybe you had gotten shot."

"Yeah, I'm fine," Trisha took off her black snow hat and let her purple hair fall down around her face. "That must have looked pretty scary. I just tripped on a tree root that was sticking out of the ground."

"I hope that old coot didn't recognize you," Janea said in a shaky voice.

"I'm sure he didn't," Hailey said flippantly. "Everything's cool. He can't prove a thing."

With that, everyone started laughing and talking about his or her adventure, everyone that is except Kayla. She sat huddled in the corner of the back seat…shivering.

Chapter 14
Confession

Kayla tried to fall asleep as she stared at the stars through the skylight in Hailey's room. She had such an unsettling feeling. She wasn't sure where she belonged anymore. She wasn't sure who she was anymore. She pulled her sleeping bag up tight against her chest, trying to take away the chill she still felt.

It wasn't like her to be disrespectful to teachers, not to mention stooping to vandalism. Once she had even helped her neighborhood clean up some graffiti at their local park in Riverside. Things were all so complicated now. Before, she thought being a Christian just meant believing in God, going to church, and being a good person. The words came back to her she had heard at church on Wednesday night, "even the demons believe in God and shudder."

Another chill went through her whole body. She glanced around the room. Hailey's deep breathing assured Kayla she was out. Trisha and Janea were sleeping on the floor with Kayla, and they both seemed to be sound asleep.

Kayla wanted to talk to someone, to sort out everything she was feeling. She remembered how Pastor Ryan had talked to God so easily at dinner. She decided to give it a try, so with some hesitancy, she whispered her first truly heartfelt prayer to God. "Lord, I have believed in You for as long as I can remember, but I have never really given You complete control of my life." A small tear escaped her eye and trickled down her cheek. "I guess when You took Dad home to be with You, I kind of stopped trusting You like I did when I was little. The truth is, I just didn't understand." Kayla remembered back to the day when Dad had died. Her whole world was shaken. In a way, her faith in God was so reliant upon him, that once he was gone, she had nothing left.

"I still miss him," she continued her prayer, "but I am choosing to trust You with my life. I am so ashamed of what I've done tonight. Please forgive me…I need You. I want to give You all of my life, and I want to live like You want me to."

Kayla felt an immediate peace settle over her. She knew God had heard her, and forgiven her. In a way, she felt like this was a whole new beginning for her. She stared deep into the night sky; suddenly, a new feeling of warmth swept over her. The sky no longer held the scary vastness it did when she was out earlier. The stars seemed like pinholes in the darkness, letting God's light shine through. Excitement about her newfound faith rushed through her. What a wonderful thing to feel so loved. Soon, new thoughts started filtrating through her mind. She was not used to listening to God's voice, but somehow she knew He was speaking to her. The thought came to her that the Bible says God is her Father. She was not fatherless. Anything she needed, He would always be right there to listen.

She looked over at Hailey once more. In a way she felt sorry for her. She had never even met her father, and her mom didn't seem to be there for her either. Mom would never just leave Kayla with someone who didn't pay any attention to her like Diane had done. The memory of toilet papering Mr. Bradford's house came flooding back to her. Suddenly Kayla's conscience pricked her heart, and she knew she needed to make things right with him.

The next morning, as she rode home with Mom and Cole, they drove past Mr. Bradford's house.

Mom exclaimed, "Oh my goodness, who would do such a thing. Kids these days." Kayla couldn't handle it, she blurt out her whole experience last night, even her talk with God. She also told Mom about cheating on the history quiz. Mom was quiet at first, but then she said, "It sounds like you have done a lot of growing up this weekend. I know this might sound strange coming from a parent after a night like you had, but I am proud of you."

Kayla didn't know what to say. Somehow, telling Mom was giving her more courage to tell Mr. Bradford. "I am going to go over to Mr. Bradford's house today and help him clean up," she said.

Cole broke into the conversation, "I think she should get in big trouble," he said with a goofy grin.

"Cole!" Kayla exclaimed, knowing her little brother was just teasing her.

"Well," Mom said, "even though I am proud of you for deciding to give your life completely to God, you're still going to be our dishwasher for the next month."

Kayla gave a playful moan. In truth, she was really happy with how her family was growing. They may not have Dad anymore, but God was with them, and He was helping each of them through their daily lives. He had helped Cole to make some new friends, He had helped Mom overcome her fear, and He had helped her to see that doing what God says is more important than being popular.

"Oh, I talked to Nana," Mom said, "and she said she has been praying God would show her what to do about her loneliness. When I asked her if she wanted to move in with us, she said it was God's answer to her prayers."

Kayla couldn't believe her ears, "You mean she is actually going to move in with us? When?"

"Well, I'm not sure exactly when, but I think she wants to move in as soon as possible."

Kayla felt so good, she almost forgot about the task before her, but when they pulled into the driveway, Mom was quick to remind her.

"How long do you think you will be at Mr. Bradford's house?" She asked.

Kayla sighed deeply before answering, "As long as it takes to clean up that mess." She wrinkled up her nose at the thought.

By the time she rode her bike over to Mr. Bradford's house. He was already outside cleaning up the mess. Kayla approached him cautiously; she still couldn't get the picture out of her mind of him coming after them with a shotgun. He looked up at her and she once again felt frozen to the spot she was standing on. "Lord, help me," she silently prayed.

A few moments passed before she finally found her tongue. "I came by to apologize for this mess," she said barely above a whisper, "and to help you clean it up."

Mr. Bradford looked at her a little stunned. "You mean to tell me you toilet papered my house, and now you want to clean it up? That doesn't sound like very good planning on your part." Kayla couldn't tell, but it almost looked like a smile was playing at the corner of his lips.

"It wasn't exactly my plan," Kayla said trying to keep her gaze steady. "I was with some friends..." Kayla quickly changed her statement, trying not to give Hailey away. "I mean I realized I made a huge mistake, so I decided to come over today and ask for your forgiveness."

"Well, I must say, I was pretty upset," Mr. Bradford said furrowing his brow, "but I am impressed at your courage in confessing to me. So, I'll tell you what. If you help me clean up today, and then come over once a week for a month to help with yard work, I will not bother to get the school or your parents involved. If I find out who the other people are though, I will not be so generous to them."

"Thank you, Mr. Bradford, but I already told my mom. It looks like I am going to keep pretty busy this month with yard work for you and dishes every night at home." With that, they both laughed and then got to work. Kayla felt like she was a part of an environmental clean up crew. It wasn't the most fun way to spend her Saturday afternoon, but she did learn a few interesting facts about her history teacher. She learned he boils his weeds instead of using chemical poisons, (a relief to Kayla who was still not totally over her "poisoning" experience with Pastor Ryan), he had never paddled a student, and the gun he had last night was not loaded.

Chapter 15
Confrontation

It was almost four o'clock before she started to ride her bike home from Mr. Bradford's house. On her way, she decided to stop by Sara's house to tell her everything that happened so far this weekend.

Sara came to the door wearing a light green, spaghetti strap dress. It brought out her green eyes, and her long, curly red hair made her look like an angel as the sun shone on it.

"Come in," Sara said when she saw Kayla. I am just getting ready to go to Main Street Grill with my family. They are having this great concert there tonight. Jimmy is going to play a few songs as well; do you want to come with us?"

"I don't know," Kayla said, "after what I have to say, I don't know if you will still want me to come." It struck her how nice Sara had been to her all along. Hailey was outright rude to Sara, but she never said anything negative to Kayla about hanging out with her. "First," Kayla started out as they made their way to Sara's room, "I want to apologize for not being a very good friend to you."

Sara turned to stare at Kayla, "What are you talking about? You're new, and..."

"I know, I know," Kayla cut her off, "but you have been so nice to me, and I am so embarrassed, but I believed some of the rumors Hailey spread about you. Well, I didn't believe them at first, but then I saw your dad buying poison at the store, and one thing led to another. Before I knew it, I was in the kitchen with him, trying to protect my lemonade." Kayla let out a little laugh, and Sara's eyes got as big as saucers.

"You mean that's why you went into the kitchen? Did you say anything to my dad?"

"No, I felt really foolish, and decided I would be better off not to taste the lemonade. Then your dad said that sincere prayer and I saw how loving your family was. Then your dad told the story about how he had bought poison for the rats. That's when I saw how ridiculous the thought of him being a murderer was. I am so sorry, and I just wanted to come by to tell you I am so thankful for that night, and how your family shared its love so freely with me. It's been a long time since I have been at the table with a complete family." Kayla blinked hard, trying to control her tears, and then she stood up to leave.

"Where are you going?" Sara asked.

"I thought I would go home and get cleaned up."

"Why are you covered in dirt anyway?"

"It's a long story," Kayla said.

Sara giggled, "That's what friends are for, listening to the long stories of life, and accepting us for who we are." She leaned over and gave Kayla a big hug. "I'm glad you are able to see past the rumors about me and my family. Hey, do you want some lemonade?" she asked with a grin.

"You know what, I think I do," Kayla said, relief flooding her. Sara still wanted to be her friend.

"Great, I'll be right back." Sara quickly returned with two tall glasses of lemonade, and some crackers and cheese.

"Why would Hailey make up such a crazy rumor about your dad anyway?" Kayla asked, after she had explained her whole experience with Hailey and then her heart to heart with God after the T.P. incident.

"Well, it goes way back to when Dad and Dianne were in high school. They dated their junior year, you know."

"No way!"

"Yeah, it's pretty freaky. Anyway, Dad broke up with her, because she was totally into herself. They used to go to the same church, but

Dianne has never gone to church again, and she's never forgiven him. After high school, she married a rich guy when Dad was in Bible college. That's where he met Mom. Anyway, just after she had Hailey, she divorced him, taking most of his wealth. Hailey has just caught her mom's bitterness.

"Wow, so is that the reason Hailey doesn't like you?"

"I think so, but there are a lot of people who make up rumors about pastors. I have just learned to ignore most of them." Both girls finished up their snack, and then Kayla called Mom to see if she could go with the Smiths to Main Street Grill. Mom said sure, so Sara took Kayla over to her closet to pick out something to wear.

"Can I borrow this red flutter sleeve dress?"

"Sure," Sara answered, and then she showed Kayla where the shower was for her to get ready.

By six 'o clock, both girls were ready, complete with new manicures and pedicures. Kayla had so much fun getting ready with Sara. Sara had a whole drawer full of nail polish. Kayla had chosen to do her nails in a French manicure, and Sara had done hers in a green color that matched her dress.

"It's time to go, Elizabeth hollered to the girls, and then they all loaded up into the Smith's big blue van. Kayla sat next to Justin.

"You girls sure look spiffy today," Justin said, and Kayla could feel her cheeks turn red. She wondered what he saw in Hailey; besides the fact she was beautiful. Or maybe he had never called her in the first place. Hailey was good at making up stories.

Before long, they were all climbing out of the van. Kayla noticed how Pastor Ryan opened the door for Elizabeth. She silently hoped her future husband would be that kind of a gentleman.

They could hear the music playing as they walked toward the door. Justin saw a group of his friends and quickly vanished into the crowd.

"Isn't this place cool?" Sara said as her parents headed for a booth in the back, leaving them standing near the entrance.

"Yeah, I love the decorations," Kayla said as they both scanned the room to see where they wanted to sit. Sara spotted Tyler and Josh and pointed to where they were sitting, just as Kayla saw Hailey approaching them. Oh, no, she thought.

"Oh, if it isn't goody two shoes and her sidekick," Hailey said with both hands on her hips. "You know, it isn't Christmas." Kayla looked down at her red dress then at Sara's green dress.

"Trisha said she saw you helping Mr. Bradford clean up this morning! How could you? Did you rat on me too?"

"No," Kayla defended herself. "It was wrong of us to toilet paper his house. I went back to apologize, but I didn't tattle on you."

Hailey scowled at Sara, and then looked at Kayla with a challenge in her eyes. "I will give you one more chance. Ditch the goody two shoes, and join our table."

"Hailey, I'm sorry I ever followed you in the first place," Kayla said. "I want to be your friend, but not at the cost of my integrity."

Hailey glared at Kayla, and then stormed back to her booth in the corner with Trisha and Janea.

"Can you believe her?" Kayla said as tears started trickling down her cheeks. She quickly headed for the bathroom before anyone could notice.

Sara was right behind her. Luckily, the bathroom was empty.

"Are you O.K?" Sara asked while Kayla grabbed some tissue.

"Yeah," she said in between sniffles. "I am just not used to dealing with people like her. How can you be so nice to her when she is so mean?"

"Well, Mom has always taught me we are to love our enemies. It is easier said than done though. I guess I try to understand why people are the way they are. Hailey is insecure and bitter. So, I just pray for her a lot, and I think God helps me to love her."

"I wish there was more we could do to help people like her. I wish everyone could be a Christian."

"Maybe we could start praying together for people like her," Sara said while Kayla used a paper towel to dry her eyes. "I know of a coffee shop some people from church own. It is called Holy Grounds. We could meet there before school to pray."

Kayla liked the idea. "Yeah, we could be like undercover agents scouting out the school for people who need to be prayed for. No, not undercover agents, undercover angels!" With that, both girls burst out laughing. It felt so good to Kayla to have a real friend.

"Do you want to see if Josh and Tyler have any room at their table?" Sara asked, with a twinkle in her eye.

"Are you asking for me, or do you have a particular reason you want to sit there?" Kayla asked, "Maybe a particular reason named Josh?"

Sara blushed slightly, "We are all friends, and I think we should keep it that way," she said, but she didn't sound too convincing.

After Kayla made herself presentable again, both girls walked out of the bathroom arm in arm with big smiles on their faces. Kayla followed Sara to the booth Josh and Tyler were sitting in.

"Is there room for us?" Sara asked.

"Sure," Tyler said as he scooted over so they could sit down. "Isn't this concert amazing?" Kayla hadn't been paying too much attention to the actual music, since she was so busy thinking about Hailey. She looked up towards the stage. The band was good, she thought.

"Look," Sara said, "Jimmy's getting ready to play next." Kayla looked over at Jimmy who was tuning his guitar. She glanced once again at Hailey and her friends. They were sitting quietly listening to the concert. She looked at Tyler and Josh. Josh was watching Tyler pretend to play drums with two straws. Sara was laughing. Kayla sighed deeply. "Thank You, Lord, for helping me to get through the first couple weeks of seventh grade, and to make some great friends."

UNDERCOVER ANGELS/Book #2

The Oregon Caves Trip

Coming Soon…

For details visit:
www.angeladusenberry.com

CPSIA information can be obtained at www.ICGtesting.com
Printed in the USA
270649BV00005B/4/P